The Fairy House
Fairies to the Rescue

Welcome to the Fairy House –
a whole new magical world...

Have you got all *The Fairy House* books?

- ☐ FAIRY FRIENDS
- ☐ FAIRY FOR A DAY
- ☐ FAIRIES TO THE RESCUE
- ☐ FAIRY RIDING SCHOOL
- ☐ FAIRY SLEEPOVER
- ☐ FAIRY JEWELS
- ☐ FAIRY PARTY
- ☐ FAIRY FLYING LESSONS

Make sure you visit www.thefairyhouse.co.uk
for competitions, prizes and lots more fairy fun!

The Fairy House
Fairies to the Rescue

Kelly McKain

Illustrated by Nicola Slater

SCHOLASTIC

To Lucy and Maria, with love

First published in the UK in 2007 by Scholastic Children's Books
An imprint of Scholastic Ltd
Euston House, 24 Eversholt Street
London, NW1 1DB, UK
Registered office: Westfield Road, Southam, Warwickshire, CV47 0RA
SCHOLASTIC and associated logos are trademarks and or registered trademarks of Scholastic Inc.
This edition published in 2009

ISBN 978 1 407 10888 9

A CIP catalogue record for this book is available from the British Library

Printed in the UK by CPI Bookmarque, Croydon, CR0 4TD
Papers used by Scholastic Children's Books are made
from wood grown in sustainable forests.

1 3 5 7 9 10 8 6 4 2

This is a work of fiction. Names, characters, places, incidents and dialogues
are products of the author's imagination or are used fictitiously. Any resemblance
to actual people, living or dead, events or locales is entirely coincidental.

www.kellymckain.co.uk
www.scholastic.co.uk/zone

Chapter 1

When Katie arrived at the Fairy House on Friday night after school, she got a lovely surprise. Her fairy friends had made a slide from twigs woven together with long grass, going from Daisy's bedroom window to the tree roots below. As Katie arrived, Rosehip was careering down it, crying, "Wheeeeee!" As she landed at the bottom and smiled up at Katie, Snowdrop appeared at the window, ready for her turn.

"Oh, wow! This is amazing!" Katie cried, running to the door and grabbing the sparkly blue handle, which Bluebell had bewitched with fairy dust. "I believe in fairies, I believe in fairies, I believe in fairies," she whispered, as fast as she could. She squealed with delight as the top of her head tingled, and with a great whooshing sound roaring in her ears she felt herself shrinking to fairy size. Then she raced into the house, calling, "Hi, I'm here! Can I have a go?"

She dashed upstairs, past Bluebell's beautiful pressed-flower pictures on the walls, into Daisy's bedroom, which they'd painted a cheery sunshine yellow. She gave Daisy and Bluebell a big hug, and they watched Snowdrop go sliding down, laughing all the way, her

long black hair streaming out behind her.

"I made the slide!" said Bluebell proudly. "And you're next!"

Katie squealed with delight as she  went whizzing down, and all the fairies cheered her on. At the bottom, she caught her breath and Rosehip and Snowdrop pulled her into a hug. She thought again how lucky she was to have the most wonderful friends in the whole world.

When Katie had accidentally left her dolls' house outside under the oak tree one night, she'd never dreamt that *fairies* would move in. In fact, she'd thought they only existed in stories, not in real life, and when she'd first met them she hadn't quite believed her eyes! But here they were – fragile, shy little Snowdrop, with her tumbling black hair and silky petal skirt; bold Bluebell with her striking blue bob and cheeky smile; flame-haired Rosehip who loved song and dance; and kind, gentle Daisy, with her yellow plaits and cheerful nature.

Daisy and Bluebell came whizzing down the slide then and all four fairies gathered excitedly around Katie.

"Tomorrow's Saturday, isn't it?" asked Snowdrop breathlessly. "That means no school, doesn't it?"

"We can play together all day," added Rosehip, fluttering into the air with excitement and turning a few cartwheels. "If it's sunny again we can lie out on the roof and make up stories and tell jokes and whisper secrets and –"

Katie's shoulders slumped. She'd forgotten about Saturday. "I was really looking forward to spending tomorrow with you too," she told her friends sadly. "But I've got to do something horrible instead. You remember Tiffany from my class—"

The fairies all shuddered. Bluebell said, "Revolting Tiffany? How could I ever forget?"

Katie grimaced. "Yes, well, revolting Tiffany saw Mrs Borthwick praising my work when we began writing fairy tales today. We have to finish them off

for homework, but now Tiffany wants me to write her story *for* her. That's why she's coming round tomorrow morning. If she gets a star for it, her dad's promised her a pony."

The fairies' eyes grew wide with amazement.

"A pony? Just for getting one single star?" spluttered Snowdrop.

"It's not fair!" cried Rosehip crossly. "I'd love a pony!"

"Me too!" declared Bluebell, stamping her foot to prove it.

"And she's not even going to write the story herself – that's cheating!" gasped Daisy, shocked.

They all agreed that they'd love a pony and that Tiffany was horrid and lazy and didn't deserve so much as a hoof pick.

"But why did you agree?" wailed Bluebell. "Why didn't you just tell

her to go and stick her head in a bucket? That's what *I* would have done!"

"Yes, a bucket of *cold custard*," added Rosehip, and Bluebell and Snowdrop sniggered. Daisy just lowered her eyes demurely. She was never ever mean about anyone, even though Tiffany really was the most revolting girl any of them had ever met.

"I don't *want* her to come over," Katie grumbled. "But she said that if I don't help her she'll tell the nice girls in my class not to be friends with me, and she'll be an even more horrible bully to me than ever!"

"Oh, that's awful!" cried Daisy, putting her arm round her. "You poor thing."

All the fairies agreed that Katie was a poor thing, and she found eight sympathetic arms around her.

"But will you still help us with our task?" asked Snowdrop anxiously. "You know, when she's gone home?"

Katie nodded. As well as having lots of fun together, the fairies had a serious mission, given to them by the Fairy Queen, and Katie had promised to do everything she could to help them.

Snowdrop pulled the scroll from the Fairy Queen out of a pocket hidden among the petals of her skirt and unfurled it. They all peered over her shoulders and read it again:

Fairy Task No. 45826

By Royal Command of the Fairy Queen

Terrible news has reached Fairyland. As you know, the Magic Oak is the gateway between Fairyland and the human world. The sparkling whirlwind can only drop fairies off *here*. Humans plan to knock down our special tree and build a house on the land. If this happens, fairies will no longer be able to come and help people and the environment. You must stop them from doing this terrible thing and make sure that the tree is protected for the future. Only then will you be allowed back into Fairyland.

By order of Her Eternal Majesty
The Fairy Queen

PS You will need one each of the twelve birthstones to work the magic that will save the tree - but hurry, there's not much time!

The Magic Oak was the very tree that the Fairy House stood under. And with Katie's help the fairies had already got two of the birthstones. The first had been easy – Katie's ring from Auntie Jane was set with a garnet. And by a stroke of luck they'd found the second, topaz, at school when Bluebell had turned big and taken Katie's place in class. That day the revolting Tiffany had also revealed that her father, Max Towner, was the property tycoon who built Katie's little close of new houses. He was also the very man planning to knock down the tree and build a luxury home in the almost-meadow.

If he succeeded, it would spell disaster for both earth *and* Fairyland. No one knew exactly what would happen if fairies couldn't come to

earth and look after the plants and animals any more, but they knew it wouldn't be good. And without their special tasks to do on earth, who knew what would become of the fairy people? It was safe to say that the future of Fairyland, and maybe earth too, depended on the five friends.

Snowdrop pointed to the PS. "There's not much time – and we've only got two birthstones so far." Her eyes filled with panic. "What if the diggers come and we're not ready and—"

Katie took hold of her pale, trembling hands and tried to smile. "As soon as Tiffany's gone tomorrow I'll come and see you, and we can work out how to get another birthstone," she promised. Then she gave them all a stern look.

"But while she's here you *must* stay out of the way," she warned, "especially you, Bluebell. And don't worry. I won't be bringing her anywhere near the Fairy House."

"But surely it doesn't matter if we hover around," Rosehip reasoned. "She won't be able to see us."

People could only see the fairies if they believed in them, and as most children and all adults didn't, they were usually fairly safe from being spotted.

"But she might believe," said Katie. "I don't really want to find out, do you?"

The fairies all shook their heads in alarm. Tiffany was so horrible, who knew *what* she might do if she got hold of them.

Just then, Katie heard Mum calling her in for tea.

"Come straight back out afterwards!" cried Bluebell, beaming. "We can play on the slide and—"

"I can't," Katie said regretfully. "Mum's really excited about Tiffany coming over. She thinks she's a real friend of mine and so she's insisting we make a cake for her."

Bluebell stamped her foot. "She gets a cake too!" she grumbled. "So unfair! Why can't your mum make one for us? We're your *real* friends!"

Katie smiled sadly. "I wish I could introduce you all to her," she said, "but she doesn't believe in fairies. I did try to tell her about you but she just

13

thought I'd made you up as a game."

"Oh, OK," said Bluebell regretfully.

So Katie hugged her friends goodbye, took hold of the doorknob and chanted the magic words. As soon as she was big again, she swished away through the tall grass and wild flowers. "I'll see you tomorrow – as soon as I can," she called back over her shoulder.

"Not if we see you sooner!" replied Rosehip, and she and Bluebell giggled a naughty giggle.

But Katie was ducking under the garden fence, too far away to hear.

At the tea table, Katie pushed her green beans miserably around her plate as Mum talked excitedly about her "new friend" coming over.

"So what are you girls planning to do?" she asked again, as Katie hadn't answered the first time.

Katie pulled on a smile – she hated to hurt Mum's feelings. "We're going to make up fairy stories," she said, "and then write them in our neat work books to show Mrs Borthwick."

"What a good idea!" Mum exclaimed. "With your imagination I'm sure you'll come up with something wonderful."

"Hmm," Katie mumbled. Once again, she thought how lucky she was to have the loveliest mum in the world. She suddenly wished that she could tell the truth about Tiffany, but she knew Mum would be furious and cancel the story writing session. She'd probably tell Mrs Borthwick about Tiffany's

demands too, and Tiffany would get into trouble at school. And that would make her more horrid to Katie than ever.

No, Katie knew she'd just have to smile sweetly and put up with Tiffany for the day. She thought she could manage it – she just hoped that her fairy friends would behave themselves too!

 Chapter 2

On Saturday morning, Katie was getting ready when the four fairies fluttered in her open bedroom window.

"That's a pretty dress," said Snowdrop approvingly.

"And lovely sandals," added Bluebell.

Katie smiled wryly. "Thanks. But don't think I've forgotten that I told you to stay down in the almost-meadow!"

Daisy blushed. "I know," she mumbled, "but Bluebell and Rosehip persuaded us to come with them."

Katie raised an eyebrow at the two naughtiest fairies. "Oh, you did, did you?" she said.

"We didn't want to leave you all alone with that horrid girl!" Bluebell said, huffily.

"I don't want to be alone with her either!" cried Katie. "But what if she sees you? She's the last person I'd want to find out about you. She could be dangerous!"

"We'll hide, we're brilliant at keeping out of sight since we spent a whole day at school," Rosehip insisted, ducking behind the curtain to prove it.

The curtain billowed in the breeze, revealing her, and they all laughed.

"Well, obviously I'll find a much better hiding place than that," she said crossly. "That was only for a demonstration!"

Katie couldn't deny that the fairies had kept out of sight at school – hiding behind maths books, making graph paper disguises and using paint palettes as camouflage. "OK," she said reluctantly, "but *please* be careful!"

"We promise," they chanted together.

"Fairies' honour." And they did a strange little salute to prove it.

Suddenly the doorbell rang, making the fairies jump. Katie took a deep breath. "Gotta go," she said. "That'll be Tiffany."

By the time Katie got downstairs Mum had welcomed Tiffany in and was offering her a drink.

"Get me fizzy pop," ordered Tiffany, without so much as a please or a thank you.

Mum smiled, a little tightly. "We don't have that, I'm afraid," she said. "How about orange juice?"

"Yum, yum, yes please!" said Katie, trying to make up for Tiffany's rudeness.

"That will do, I *suppose*," Tiffany grumbled.

But when Mum brought the orange juice through to the living

room it turned out that it wouldn't do at all.

"It's got bits in!" Tiffany accused, giving Mum a reproachful look, as though she were trying to poison her.

Luckily Mum laughed. "They're bits of *orange*!" she said. "How can you mind that?"

Katie laughed too . . . and then she heard chuckling behind her, like tinkling bells. She made herself stay still and not look around. She knew that the fairies had flown in the living room window – and after she'd told them to stay out of sight too!

Mum didn't seem to hear them, but unfortunately Tiffany *did*.

"What's that noise?" she demanded.

"Nothing," said Katie firmly, then, while Tiffany was busy staring into her glass with disgust, she quickly glanced at the fairies, giving them a warning look.

"I want something else to drink—" Tiffany began.

"Come up to my bedroom," Katie interrupted, hurrying her into the hallway. She didn't want Tiffany to see her private things, but then, she didn't want her to upset Mum either. Not when she'd been out to buy the orange juice specially.

When they reached Katie's doorway, Tiffany peered inside and said, "Is this it? Seriously?"

Katie nodded, biting her lip, vowing not to let this rude girl bother her.

"Pah!" Tiffany snorted. "I thought

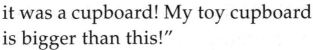

it was a cupboard! My toy cupboard is bigger than this!"

Katie saw the fairies flutter in through the bedroom window and whip behind a bookshelf. They poked their heads round her *Illustrated Treasury of Fairy Stories*, smiling cheekily.

Just then, Tiffany did a big yawn without covering her mouth, revealing bits of her breakfast still stuck in her teeth. Forgetting themselves, the fairies all shrieked

"Yuck!" and Tiffany whirled around and caught sight of Snowdrop's glimmering wing bobbing back behind the book.

Katie's heart began to thud. What if she'd seen her?

"Argh!" Tiffany was yelling. "There's some big insect thing in here! Let's whack it with a book!" She grabbed the *Illustrated Treasury of Fairy Tales* and whirled it round her head. Luckily the four fairies zoomed out of the window before she could see them, or worse, *splat* them!

"You're right, it *was* an insect, and I just saw it go out," Katie said, marching to the window and slamming it shut. "That'll make sure it doesn't come back in."

Katie breathed out. Phew – that was close!

Tiffany dropped Katie's book on

the floor, and Katie winced as it landed open, bending the pages and crunching the spine. "What games have you got?" Tiffany demanded.

With a sigh, Katie cast her eyes up at her shelves. "Erm, Guess Who, Cluedo, Operation," she began.

"I meant *computer* games," Tiffany interrupted, rolling her eyes. "Don't tell me you haven't even got a computer! Honestly, Katie, your life really *is* as boring as I imagined!"

Furious, Katie screwed up her fists and turned to the window to avoid Tiffany's eye. Rosehip and Bluebell were standing on the sill, trying to heave it open. They hated being left out of things, even things as hideous as having to entertain Tiffany. But seeing them cheered Katie up. Her life wasn't dull at all. In fact, it was full of fairy magic!

"Well, then, let's get on with the homework so I can leave as soon as possible," grumbled Tiffany.

"Fine by me!" said Katie cheerfully. "Come on, we can do your story in the living room."

This time she galloped down the stairs as fast as she could. As they sat down at the table, Katie was pleased to see that the fairies were outside, and having far too much fun to think about causing trouble with Tiffany. Bluebell and Rosehip were in fits of giggles, hanging by their knees from the rotary washing line in the back garden, which

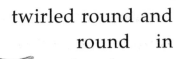

twirled round and round in the breeze. Snowdrop was balancing on one of the lines, pretending to be a gymnast, and Daisy was lazing in a hammock made from Mum's bikini top. Katie reluctantly pulled her gaze back from the window.

"Right, make up my story," Tiffany ordered. "I want to be a princess, and not one of those silly poor ones who knows when there's a pea under their mattress. I want to be a rich, beautiful one with loads of dresses and shoes. No peas – got it?"

Katie sighed. "Once upon a time. . ." she began.

Tiffany just copied down every word she said, hardly even listening. Poor Katie hated being forced to come up with ideas about Princess Tiffany being adored by everyone and marrying a lovely prince. She'd far rather have written about Nasty Tiffany who got thrown into a deep, dark pit with lots of hungry wolves, no, make that snakes, no actually, make that wolves *and* snakes! But she knew that if she did that Tiffany would only force her to rewrite it and end up staying longer – and Katie certainly wasn't keen on that!

After a long while, and with the story nearly finished, Mum wandered in to ask if they'd like a sandwich.

"Yes, I want cream cheese and smoked salmon on white bread with the crusts cut off," Tiffany demanded, without even looking up from her neat work book.

Mum raised her eyebrows at Katie and told Tiffany that there was tuna and cucumber or ham and tomato.

Once again, Katie wished she could explain to Mum that Tiffany wasn't *really* her friend, but she knew it would only make things worse.

Over lunch, Tiffany picked the cucumber out of her sandwich and pointedly left the crusts. But when Mum brought out the home-made chocolate cake she and Katie had baked the night before, her mean little eyes lit up.

If *Katie* had left half her lunch, Mum would have said, "No dessert for you, madam." But because

Tiffany was a guest she still got a slice of cake. She tucked in noisily, then grinned at Mum and said the cake was quite tasty, considering it wasn't from a shop. Katie thought that maybe Tiffany had decided to be nice at last, but she was wrong. Now that the story was written and she'd got what she wanted, she began pulling mean faces at Katie when Mum wasn't looking.

Trying to ignore her, Katie gazed out of the window. Startled, she noticed that the fairies were now watching from the washing line, and *they* certainly weren't ignoring her! Instead they were pulling rude faces back, waggling their fingers and sticking out their tongues. Katie

spluttered with laughter, then clamped her hand over her mouth. When Tiffany demanded to know what was so funny she just shook her head and said, "Nothing."

Tiffany scoffed her slice of cake in record time (while making horrible squelchy noises and chewing with her mouth open) and then stared at the rest of it so hard that Mum eventually offered her another piece. When that was gone, she helped herself to more without even asking.

When Katie had finished her slice, she sneaked a glance at the washing line. But the fairies weren't there. She squinted out into the sunlight, searching the blue sky for them. But they were nowhere in sight.

Just then she felt a tug on her

ponytail. Someone was climbing up it as if it were one of the ropes in PE. Katie heard a small tinkling voice in her ear – the climber-upper was Rosehip! "Hmm, rotten fish, overcooked sprouts and smelly trainers, I think!" she whispered.

Katie couldn't ask what she meant, of course, but she had a feeling the fairies were up to something. Then she caught a glimpse of Bluebell zooming across the ceiling and shaking some fairy dust down on to the table. It landed, a just-visible sparkly sheen, on the last piece of cake.

Seeing that Katie was looking at the cake, Tiffany grabbed it and stuffed it into her mouth.

Katie knew she should have stopped her, but she was far too keen to see what would happen.

What happened was, Tiffany chewed for a moment, then her usually pink face went from red to grey to almost green, and she bounced up and down in her chair, her eyes bulging. Then she spat the cake out with a great shout of "Bleugh!!!!" and dashed off to the loo.

"Oh dear, poor thing," said Mum. "She obviously had a little too much."

Hiding her grin, Katie asked to leave the table and went outside. Round the corner by the water barrel she burst out laughing. The fairies gathered round her, their chuckles chiming like tiny bells. They looked very pleased with themselves!

"Now, that was very silly," Katie began, trying to keep a straight face. "What if she'd spotted you?"

"But she didn't," said Rosehip.

"And it *did* serve her right," reasoned Snowdrop.

"And it *was* very funny!" Bluebell giggled.

Katie couldn't help smiling. "Yes, it was," she admitted. "But now you really have to go home. Tiffany will be gone soon and I'll come and meet you at the Fairy House."

But the fairies still looked reluctant. "Can't we stay a little longer?" pleaded Bluebell. "I was planning to fire clods of cut grass at her out of your mum's bikini top."

"Don't you dare!" cried Katie, though secretly she thought it was a rather good idea. "*Please* go home now. It's for your own safety. I'll get

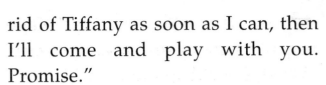

rid of Tiffany as soon as I can, then I'll come and play with you. Promise."

"Can we do skipping?" asked Snowdrop hopefully.

"Of course!" Katie replied.

That did the deal and the four fairies flew off towards the almost-meadow, spinning and turning in the air, still giggling over their trick. Katie waved them off, then she went back in to find Tiffany standing in the kitchen, drinking the orange juice, bits and all. Anything to get rid of the taste of rotting fish, overcooked sprouts and smelly trainers!

Chapter 3

When Tiffany had recovered from the fairies' little trick, she insisted on calling her nanny to come and take her home.

At last! thought Katie excitedly. In half an hour she'd be back at the Fairy House, making up skipping chants with her *real* friends.

Mum sent them both out to play in the garden while they waited for the car to arrive.

Katie suggested that they do

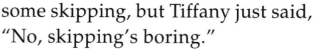

some skipping, but Tiffany just said, "No, skipping's boring."

"Well, what if we –" Katie began, but she soon stopped short, stiffening. Tiffany had noticed the almost-meadow beyond the garden. She lumbered across the lawn, shouting, "Come on, let's go exploring!"

Katie stared in horror. She couldn't let Tiffany go into the almost-meadow. What if she spotted the Fairy House? She had to think of an excuse – and fast! "Come back!" she called. "We can't go without Mum's permission."

"Goody-goody two shoes!" Tiffany taunted, forcing herself through the thin wire fence.

Katie had no choice but to go after her, feet flying and heart pounding. Tiffany ran straight to the oak tree

and gave it a hefty kick just to be horrid, then she bobbed down beside the Fairy House.

Katie felt sick. "Stop it!" she cried as Tiffany picked it up and shook it about. Katie wanted to wrestle it out of her grip, but she was worried that they'd end up dropping it.

After a few heart-stopping seconds, Tiffany put it back down with a thud and clicked the catch open. Katie held her breath as the whole front of the house swung open like a book, revealing all the rooms inside.

What if her friends were revealed too?

Katie peered into the house, hardly daring to breathe. But there wasn't a fairy in sight, thank goodness! She was just wondering where they could be when she spotted a sliver of Snowdrop's skirt sticking out of her wardrobe door. She realized that her friends had taken refuge in their hide-and-seek places. Tiffany peered into the bathroom and idly flicked the sink out on to the grass, then the loo. "Is this boring old thing yours then?" she asked.

Katie nodded, clenching her fists. Thank goodness Bluebell had found somewhere better to hide than the bath this time! She knew she had to stay calm and act as though the Fairy House really *was* just a boring old thing. Maybe then Tiffany would lose interest in it.

"I don't like what you've done inside, with all those leaves and petals and things," Tiffany announced. "I could make it much better."

Just then Katie caught a glimpse of Bluebell creeping out of the kitchen cupboard and zooming through the window. She winked at Katie and put her finger across her lips. The next moment, she was in the tall grass around Tiffany's legs, making an angry buzzing sound. Tiffany started leaping about,

shouting, "Bee! Bee!" and then she screeched as Bluebell gave her shin a sharp poke with a twig. "Ow, ow, I've been stung!' she screamed. "Let's get back inside. I hate nature!"

"Whatever you say, Tiffany," Katie said, stifling a giggle. As they walked away, with Tiffany limping dramatically, she looked back and saw her four friends sitting on the Fairy House roof, laughing.

A loud impatient *beep-beep!* filled the air as they reached the garden.

"That sounds like your lift," said Katie, with relief.

Once indoors, Tiffany shoved her neat work book into her bag and left without even saying goodbye to Katie or "thank you for having me" to Mum.

"Well, she's, erm—" Mum began.

"Nice? Yes, she is," Katie finished quickly, avoiding Mum's eye. She wished once again that she could tell her the truth about

Tiffany, but it was impossible. Instead she gave her a big hug and they wandered back into the kitchen, where Mum washed up the lunch things and Katie helped with the drying.

Afterwards, she hurried back down and out into the garden, under the wire and through the almost-meadow, calling, "Great thinking on the pretend bumblebee, Bluebell. It was a bit naughty but she really deserved it!"

But no one answered.

And when she reached the oak tree she got a terrible shock.

She stared at the ground where the Fairy House should have been. But it wasn't there!

Katie stared at the bare tree roots, completely confused. Just then three sobbing fairies crept out from under

a dock leaf. They were too upset to fly, so Katie scooped them up into her arms. "What's happened?" she gasped.

"She sneaked back here through the alleyway at the end of the street," Snowdrop blurted out. "She took our house!"

Katie hugged them all tight – she knew that Snowdrop was talking about Tiffany. "We all managed to get out—" Bluebell began.

"Thank goodness," cried Katie.

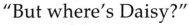

"But where's Daisy?"

"We all managed to get out, *except* Daisy," finished Rosehip. "She was still in the house – she wasn't quick enough. Tiffany's got her!"

They all began sobbing hard then, and talking at once.

Though Katie's own heart was hammering and her eyes were blurry with tears, she managed to calm them down.

"Tiffany picked up the house and we all managed to fly out of the windows," Snowdrop explained. "But then she spotted Daisy and grabbed her. It was awful – we were so scared and we didn't know what to do." And with that she burst into fresh sobs.

Rosehip put her arm round Snowdrop while Bluebell told Katie the rest of the story. She spoke

quickly, trying to beat her tears. "Luckily Rosehip had an idea. She grabbed the bottle of fairy dust from Snowdrop's pocket, and threw some back in through the window. It landed on Daisy, and she went completely rigid, like a doll. So at least Tiffany will think that's what she is and won't suspect she's a fairy."

"But Rosehip!" gasped Katie. "Now she won't have any chance of escaping!"

Rosehip looked horror-struck – she hadn't thought of that.

"Well, there's only one thing for it," said Katie firmly, "we'll have to rescue her, and quickly! She'll be trapped in Tiffany's house by now, and once that fairy dust wears off, Tiffany will realize that she's a real live fairy. Who knows what she'll do to her then?"

The three fairies all dried their eyes and blew their noses loudly on bits of dock leaf. Then Katie came up with a rescue plan – she'd tell Mum that Tiffany had left her neat work book behind (showing Mum her own instead) and ask if they could walk up to Tiffany's house to return it. Then, once inside, she'd get Daisy and the Fairy House back. The three fairies agreed that this was a very good plan indeed and that nothing in the world would stop them from coming along too.

"Let's go!" said Bluebell, zooming into the air. "Daisy needs us!" And together they hurried back to Katie's house.

As she stumbled across the almost-meadow with the three fairies flying beside her, Katie didn't

dare to imagine what terrible things Tiffany might be up to.

She just hoped they weren't already too late to save Daisy.

Chapter 4

Katie tugged at Mum's hand, pulling her faster up the street. The three fairies were riding in the pocket of her sundress, and Katie's own neat work book was clutched in her hand, the front cover facing carefully away from Mum. Mum had wanted to wait till later in the afternoon, when it wasn't so hot, but Katie had been desperate to leave straight away. Seeing how anxious she was, Mum had grabbed

her sunhat and they were out of the door in two minutes flat.

After half an hour's walk, they reached a big black iron gate. As they peered through to Tiffany's house – a huge, white villa – the

fairies peeked out of the pocket too and Katie heard Snowdrop gulp. Mum smoothed down her dress and began rummaging in her bag for a comb, but Katie said, "You can wait here if you like. I'll only be a minute."

"OK, I'll be just over there," said Mum, pointing to a nearby bench. "Be quick, darling."

Katie pressed the buzzer on the gate. After a moment it swung open and she hurried through. On tiptoes, she stretched up and banged the gold lion's-head knocker. When the tall, pale woman carrying a huge basket of laundry answered, Katie assumed she was Tiffany's mum. "Good afternoon, Mrs Towner," she said, remembering her politest manners. "Tiffany left her book at my house and I was wondering—"

The woman smiled. "Oh no, I'm not Mrs Towner," she said. "As if *she'd* bother answering the door! I'm Lisa, Tiffany's nanny."

Lisa pointed Katie in the right direction and soon she was hurrying down the long, white corridor, which was lined with gold-framed mirrors. Everything in Tiffany's house was cold and shiny and hard, and Katie almost slipped on the polished marble floor. It didn't seem like a very homely place to live.

The three fairies peeked out of her sundress pocket, already searching for Daisy. Katie could feel them beginning to fidget – they were getting more used to being indoors after going to school, but they still hated it.

After what felt like a lifetime, they

all burst into the playroom. As Tiffany looked up, the fairies bobbed down out of sight. Katie gasped as she spotted the Fairy House on the big glass table – and the awful things Tiffany had done to it.

The lovely polka-dot curtains lay in a torn heap, and the rose petal sofa covers had been replaced with scratchy black material. And the bedrooms – oh, the poor fairies! Tiffany had started painting them all in purple, then changed her mind and switched to green, but she'd been so careless that the paint had mixed together and made a hideous sludgy brown colour. The beautiful soft-glowing chain of lights Katie had helped her fairy friends to make now lay in pieces on the table, along with bits of Bluebell's pressed flower pictures.

Worst of all, Bluebell's slide, the slide they'd had so much fun on, had fallen to the floor and splintered into pieces.

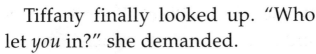

Tiffany finally looked up. "Who let *you* in?" she demanded.

"How could you?" Katie shouted.

Tiffany shrugged. "It's way better," she said matter-of-factly. "You should be *thanking* me."

Actually, Katie wished she had a wolf-and-snake pit to drop Tiffany into, but she didn't dwell on the wrecked Fairy House for long. She only cared about finding Daisy. Her eyes flicked desperately over the pile of dolls on the table, but there was no sign of her fairy friend.

Suddenly Rosehip shook at Katie's dress and pointed to a pile of the scratchy black fabric. Katie spotted Daisy, half-hidden beneath it. She hadn't recognized her at first, because the poor little fairy was not wearing her usual yellow petal skirt and daisy top, but a big orange

nylon ball gown with itchy lace at the collar and cuffs. Tiffany had also undone her plaits and scraped her hair back into a high ponytail, fixed with several big, ugly hairgrips. Even through her stiff doll's expression, Katie could tell that Daisy was thoroughly miserable, and worse – absolutely terrified.

Tiffany seemed to be playing hospitals and Katie now noticed that all the dolls had slings and head bandages and leg plasters. She breathed a sigh of relief – she was only bandaging them up – no real

harm would come to Daisy as long as she remained a doll.

Daisy met Katie's eye and managed a small desperate glance. Katie gave her a reassuring smile. But her face soon dropped – and she saw why her friend was so frightened. She stared, aghast, as Tiffany picked up a blonde doll and yanked its arm so hard that it came right off. She wasn't just bandaging her dolls up. She was giving them home-made injuries first!

Katie gaped at the blonde doll, her stomach flipping over and over.

"This fairy doll's going to have a broken wing," Tiffany announced, snatching Daisy up and turning her over and over in her sweaty pink hands. Daisy caught Katie's eye and stared at her in total terror.

Katie desperately wanted to reach

for her, but she knew she couldn't. With two of them pulling at her, poor Daisy would definitely get injured. Katie also knew that Tiffany wasn't going to just hand her over, especially if she realized how much she wanted her.

No, she'd have to be much cleverer than that.

Katie suddenly felt Bluebell and Rosehip scrabbling out of the pocket, but Snowdrop grabbed their ankles, holding them down. "Shhh! Trust Katie – she knows what she's doing," she whispered and they fell reluctantly back.

She gave Daisy a quick wink, took a deep breath to steady herself and told Tiffany, "If you're playing with *my* doll, you have to swap with me for that Miss Cassandra." She motioned to a slim plastic doll with

lots of auburn hair. "I've always wanted one," she continued, struggling to keep her voice steady. "But they're too expensive. Mum can only afford second-hand ones like that boring old thing." Hardly daring to breathe, she nodded towards Daisy. In the pocket of her sundress the three fairies crossed their fingers and squeezed their eyes tight shut, too scared to watch.

Tiffany paused over Daisy's wing and looked

at the Miss Cassandra doll, weighing it up. It was the longest moment of Katie's life.

"No," she said finally. "Don't you dare touch my Miss Cassandra! And here, have your stupid second-hand doll back!"

She hurled Daisy at Katie, who lunged to catch her, then put her straight into the pocket of the sundress where six grateful hands grabbed hold of her. A shake of fairy dust from Snowdrop brought poor Daisy back to normal and she slumped, trembling, into her friends' arms.

Chapter 5

Daisy gave Katie a gentle pinch through the fabric of her dress and said, "Pssst!"

Katie sloped over to the other side of the room, pretending to be sulking about not getting the Miss Cassandra. She glanced back but Tiffany was busy flipping through a giant wardrobe of dolls' clothes, all on hangers and with matching bags and shoes. It seemed safe to talk.

"I think I saw something," Daisy

whispered hurriedly, "something that might help with the fairy task." She turned to Bluebell. "You remember when you were big at school and Tiffany told you about her father and his plans for the almost-meadow?"

Bluebell nodded.

"Well, she said he was keeping the information about knocking down the oak tree top secret, didn't she?"

Bluebell nodded again, looking a little puzzled.

"*Well*," said Daisy excitedly, "when Tiffany stole me she sneaked into her father's study to pinch a packet of mints from his desk. While we were there I caught a glimpse of a folder sticking out from under a pile of papers. It said 'Top Secret' on it."

The other fairies and Katie were

very excited by this. They all agreed that they absolutely *had* to see what was in that folder.

"I'll create a diversion, while you two go after it," Katie told Bluebell and Rosehip, who nodded with glee. "Snowdrop, you stay here and look after Daisy," she added, and Snowdrop sighed with relief.

"Oh, and please will you get my clothes?" Daisy asked. "I feel awful in this horrid thing!" She looked down at herself and shuddered.

"No problem!" whispered Katie. "Right, let's go for it!"

Bluebell and Rosehip zoomed out of her pocket and took cover under the table.

Katie looked down at Daisy and Snowdrop.

"Hold tight, girls," she whispered. "Things might get a little bumpy!"

With that she marched up to Tiffany, finally letting all her anger out. "How *dare* you steal my dolls' house!" she shouted. "And how *could* you destroy everything we, I mean, *I* had done to it, and vandalize it into a horrible mess!"

"It looked like a dump, decorated with all those stupid twigs and leaves and stuff," Tiffany grumbled, but she seemed surprised at Katie's fierceness.

"Well, I love it!" Katie said firmly. "Besides, it's mine and I'm taking it back!"

She bundled all the things that Tiffany had broken and thrown out of the Fairy House back inside and snapped the front closed. Then she spotted Daisy's skirt, top and hair

bobbles. Quick as a flash she grabbed them and shoved them into her pocket. Katie heard Daisy whisper, "Thanks!" and two seconds later the horrid orange dress and sharp hairgrips came flying out.

Katie picked up the Fairy House and headed for the door.

"Give that here!" ordered Tiffany. "I want to keep it now I've spent ages making it better! If you take it back I'll make sure all the nice girls at school are too scared to be your friends!"

Katie whirled round in the doorway and fixed Tiffany with a steely glare. "You know what? I don't care!" she shouted. "I should never have let you come over to my house. And I wish I hadn't written your story for you. I should have

remembered that the only way to deal with bullies is to stand up to them! And that's what I'm doing right now, so there!" She gave a sharp tug on the Fairy House and it slipped from Tiffany's grasp.

"Give it baaaaaaaaaaaaack!" Tiffany wailed, just as her mother came downstairs.

"What's all this? Where's Lisa?" she demanded.

Katie couldn't help staring at Mrs Towner – she had rock solid hair fanning around her head, nails like birds' talons and the kind of clothes that teenagers usually wore.

For a moment, Katie wondered if Tiffany was going to admit to stealing the Fairy House, but of course she wasn't that honest. "Sorry, Mother," she said, pulling on a fake smile. "It's just a mix-up.

I borrowed Katie's boring old dolls' house so I could do it up nicely, as a surprise for her. But she thinks I stole it and so she came to get it back. That's why we're fighting."

Mrs Towner turned to Katie and smiled wearily. "See, dear, Tiffany didn't mean any harm," she said.

Katie clutched the Fairy House even more tightly, enraged that Mrs Towner automatically believed Tiffany. She was about to protest – loudly! – when Tiffany's mother added, "Actually, I've just been sorting through my spare jewellery box and I found this – would it do for a chandelier, girls?" She held up a blue sparkly earring, which glinted dazzlingly in the sunlight.

Katie gasped. It was made of sapphire, one of the birthstones, and

very precious. She'd had no idea how they'd ever afford one, and now it was being offered for free! Katie knew she'd have to be clever – she really had to get that gem.

She smiled and took a step towards Mrs Towner but Tiffany barged her out of the way. "Don't give it to *her*!" she snarled. "*I* should have it, I'm your daughter!"

"Now now, Tiffany," said Mrs Towner. "Don't start. It's only an odd one, you've already got a sapphire pair."

But Tiffany really didn't want

Katie to have it. "OK, I lied," she admitted. "I did steal her stupid dolls' house, and we're not really playing together at all. So you don't have to give her anything."

Katie took a deep breath and forced herself to smile. "But how could you say that when we're the best of friends?" she asked innocently. "Of course we've been playing together – if we weren't what were you doing at my house this morning?"

Tiffany looked furious. She was trapped. If she owned up about cheating on her homework she wouldn't get a pony. She'd lost and she knew it. She could only gape as her mother handed over the sapphire earring.

"Thank you very much," said Katie, then clicked the front of the

Fairy House open and hung it inside the living room. "There. It looks wonderful!"

Tiffany had absolute hysterics then, screaming, "It's not fair, *I* never get anything!"

Mrs Towner tutted at Katie, as though Tiffany's temper was all *her* fault, and swished out of the room, high heels clinking on the cold marble.

Just then, Katie spotted Bluebell and Rosehip fluttering back through the doorway, shaking their little heads sadly, as if they hadn't managed to look in the folder.

She hurriedly shut the front of the Fairy House again and made for the door but Tiffany threw herself in the way. "Oh, no, you don't!" she screeched. "Give that earring back NOW!"

"No," Katie said, calmly. "It's mine." Just then she felt Snowdrop and Daisy fly out of her pocket and she wondered what they were up to.

"Give me that house now," hissed Tiffany, "or I'll make sure you never have any friends!"

But Katie just smiled. "That's impossible," she said, "because I've already got *four* friends. Four *best* friends, in fact."

As Tiffany ranted on, singing, "Liar! Liar!" Katie caught sight of the fairies shimmering up by the ceiling. Daisy, back to normal in her cheerful clothes and plaits, was holding one of the dolls' bandages, rolled into a tight ball. Snowdrop shook a little fairy dust on to it, and the bandage grew in size until it took all four fairies to hold it.

Katie guessed what
they were up to now –
and she wasn't about to stop them!

"My friends are right here," said
Katie. "In fact, it's time for you to
meet them."

As she spoke, Rosehip and
Bluebell flew over Tiffany's head
and behind her back. Suddenly they
whipped the dolls' bandage over
her eyes.

"Help!" she
shouted. "Get off,
I can't see!" The two
little fairies giggled.
"Who's there?" she
wailed, whirling
around. "Katie?"

"Let's play hos-
pitals!" cried Bluebell. Laughing,
she began to wind the bandage
round and round her head.

"Katie, stop it!" Tiffany ordered, but the fairies kept winding the bandage until the top of her head was completely covered. She stood up and blundered around the room. "Where are you?" she demanded.

"Over here!" called Snowdrop, from the far side of the room.

"Right beside you!" Bluebell replied, tweaking Tiffany's nose.

"Down bel-o-ow!" chimed Rosehip, skimming the floor.

"And above!" added Daisy, looping the loop by the ceiling.

Katie couldn't help laughing at the fairies' trick but when Tiffany made a wild grab into the air and nearly got hold of Bluebell, she decided it was definitely time for them to leave!

Katie whistled to the fairies and they all jumped back into her

pocket, then she clicked the Fairy House shut and picked it up. "Goodbye, Tiffany," she said loudly, "and *thank you for having me*! Don't worry, I'll let myself out."

"What? Hey, come back!" shouted Tiffany, still stumbling about.

But Katie just strode up the marble corridor and out of the door.

Chapter 6

When Katie came running back out through Tiffany's black iron gates with the Fairy House clutched in her arms, Mum was very surprised. "What's going on?" she asked. Then she spotted the neat work book still tucked under Katie's elbow and suddenly understood, saying, "Tiffany's not a real friend of yours, is she?"

Katie shook her head. Mum sighed and patted the bench beside her. Katie sat down, the Fairy House

on her lap. Then she told Mum about Tiffany making her do her homework, then stealing the Fairy House and ruining the inside (though not about Daisy, of course), and about coming up with a plan to get it back.

Mum sighed and put her arm round Katie. "You should have told me she was bullying you," she said. "You can't just give in to people like that."

Katie smiled. "I know that now," she insisted. "I stood up for myself and got my things back."

"Good for you," said Mum, "but if she causes you any more trouble, promise me you'll tell me or another adult."

"I promise," said Katie solemnly.

"I'm glad she's not really your friend, though," added Mum. "The thought of that young madam coming round to our house all the time makes me shudder." Mum shuddered to demonstrate and Katie shuddered too. Then Mum shuddered an even bigger shudder and they both burst into giggles.

When they'd stopped laughing, Mum half-whispered, "I do wish you'd make a real friend, though, darling."

"I have!" Katie insisted. "In fact

I've made *four* real friends!"

Mum beamed. "Well, why not invite them round for tea sometime?"

Katie smiled. "Maybe, sometime."

"How about tomorrow?" called Bluebell from her pocket. "Then we can have cake!"

Katie couldn't help laughing out loud at that, and she had to tell Mum she was thinking of a funny thing someone had done at school.

And with that, she picked up the Fairy House and together they set off for home.

When Katie got inside, she headed straight out into the almost-meadow to put the Fairy House back where it belonged. As she swished through the tall grass, the four fairies leapt out of her pocket

and flew alongside her.

"Don't worry about not finding the Top Secret folder," she told Bluebell and Rosehip.

"Oh, we did find it, but there was only a single piece of paper inside," said Bluebell. "Nothing useful."

"It was almost blank," added Rosehip.

They both looked very disappointed.

"Hang on, what do you mean by *almost* blank?" Katie asked curiously.

"Well, when we looked more carefully, we noticed four numbers on it, one written in each corner."

Katie stopped suddenly, staring at them. "Do you remember what they were?"

"Zero, six, nine, five," said Rosehip with certainty. "Anyway, sorry we didn't find anything out."

"But you did!" Katie cried. "It could be the combination to a safe, or some kind of padlock. We'll have to see if we can work out what it's for. Well done, you two!"

Bluebell and Rosehip squealed with delight and did loop-the-loops in the air, as Snowdrop, Daisy and Katie all cheered for them.

When they reached the oak tree Katie laid the Fairy House carefully back down beneath it. Crouching down, she clutched the doorknob and whispered, "I believe in fairies, I believe in fairies, I believe in fairies." But this time she hardly noticed the crackling at the top of her head or the big whoosh as she turned small. She was the only one who'd seen what Tiffany had done to the Fairy House, and she was worried about how upset the

fairies would be when they saw it too.

They all tiptoed inside and gasped in horror at the terrible mess. Their shoulders dropped and Snowdrop wiped away a tear with her delicate hand. "Oh, how could she?" she wailed.

"It's all spoilt," cried Bluebell. "My pressed flower pictures, the rose petal sofa covers, everything!"

Just then they heard a scream from upstairs as Daisy saw what Tiffany had done to her room. "It's hideous!" she cried. "She's painted purply brown over my lovely yellow walls! And, oh! My poor Mr Sunshine!"

They all flew upstairs and dashed into Daisy's room. Her bright yellow bedspread, embroidered with a big, smiling sunshine, lay in a bundle on the floor, along with the cheery yellow spotted curtains that matched it.

Bluebell zoomed off to her room, then reappeared clutching her torn polka-dot bedspread and curtains. "Everything's ruined for ever!" she wailed.

Katie flopped down on Daisy's

bed in despair, and the fairies joined her, utterly miserable.

But after a moment, she sat bolt upright, remembering something that Mum had said. "No, it's not all ruined," she said firmly. "We can't let that bully beat us! We'll just have to put it all right again . . . and it'll be even better than before, so there!"

And with that she leapt off the bed and pulled Daisy up. "Come on," she cried. "We can mix up a new batch of yellow paint and re-do your room! And Bluebell, go and gather some more wild flowers. This time your pictures will be even more beautiful! Snowdrop, you can pick some rose petals and Rosehip, you go and choose some wild grass stalks to make rugs."

The fairies didn't look very hopeful, but they set off anyway.

Meanwhile, Katie turned big again and popped home to fetch her paints and glue and scissors and felt-tip pens and stickers and sewing kit and bag of material. Then she hurried back and tingled and whooshed down to fairy size.

Together they painted the walls and sewed up the torn bedspreads and made the dandelion and rose petals into cushions and throws, and rehung the curtains, singing as they worked. Then they gathered up a huge pile of daisies and sat outside on the bench that Bluebell had made, threading them together to make some new fairy lights.

After that, Rosehip had the idea of painting flowers all over the kitchen cupboards and Bluebell asked Snowdrop to help her make a brand-new slide, a swirly whirly one this time that twisted and turned like a helter-skelter.

"We've made the Fairy House even more beautiful than before," cried Daisy, clapping her hands. "Just as you said we would, Katie!"

Katie grinned. "Only one thing left to do," she said.

Together they took the sapphire earring down from the living room ceiling, ready to put safely in Katie's jewellery box with the other birthstones. Then they flew around the room, putting the fairy lights back up.

"Isn't it strange how things have turned out?" she mused. "I mean, I didn't want Tiffany to come over but it led to me going to her house, just when Mrs Towner had cleared out her jewellery box and found the sapphire earring. Maybe the Fairy Queen really *is* helping us with the task."

"You know, I really think she is," said Daisy, smiling.

"And that makes three birth-stones," said Bluebell proudly.

"Only nine more to find," added Rosehip, eyes shining.

"*And* we've found out Max Towner's top secret code," said Snowdrop. "Even if we don't know what it's for yet."

"And I've learned to stand up to bullies," said Katie, smiling. "You know, Tiffany may have everything she asks for, but we've got

something far better – true friendship – and I'd rather have that than all the ponies in the world!"

They all leapt up and cheered at that. Then they held hands and danced around in a big skippy circle, laughing and singing, bubbling over with happiness at being together again in their beautiful Fairy House, safely back in the almost-meadow, under the shade of the old oak tree.

**COME AND JOIN
YOUR FAIRY FRIENDS!**

For fantastic competitions,
exclusive material and lots more fairy fun,
enter the Fairy House now!

www.thefairyhouse.co.uk

Bluebell
Spring fairy

Likes:

blue, blue, blue and more blue,
turning somersaults in the air, dancing

Dislikes:

coming second, being told what to do

Daisy
Summer fairy

Likes:

everyone to be friends, bright sunshine,
cheery colours, big fairy hugs

Dislikes:

arguments, cold dark places,
orange nylon dresses

Rosehip
Autumn fairy

Likes:

riding magic ponies, telling Bluebell
what to do, playing the piano, singing

Dislikes:

keeping quiet, boring colours,
not being the centre of attention!

Snowdrop
Winter fairy

Likes:

singing fairy songs, cool quiet places, riding her
favourite magical unicorn, making snowfairies

Dislikes:

being too hot, keeping secrets

LOOK OUT FOR
BOOK FOUR!

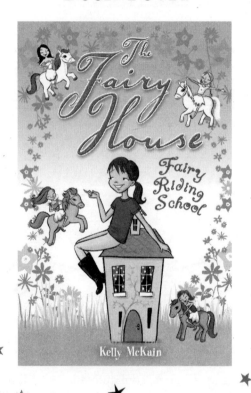